The Brechin Tales

RODERICK AND THE M

Terry Isaac

Hamish and the Marvellous Set of Bagpipes
and
Hamish and the Quest for the New Spirtle

Illustrated by Mandi Madden

ISBN 1 873891 63 6

Published by Brechin Tales Shop Ltd
Brechin House, 1 Channonry Wynd, Brechin, Angus DD9 6JS
Tel/Fax: 01356 624648
email: brechinhouse@hotmail.com

Printed by Wm Culross & Son Ltd, Coupar Angus
Tel 01828 627266 Fax 01828 627146

Hamish and the Marvellous Set of Bagpipes

The Brechin Tales

Hamish and the Marvellous Set of Bagpipes

Dedication

This tale is dedicated to children everywhere and
to the folk of Brechin City

For lovers of the flowing Scottish tune *Westering Home* I am sure that
Hamish's rendering of it played in jig time would most certainly bring tears
to the eyes. We can only conjecture as to the effect of *Westering Home* as
played by Sergeant Earnest MacBlast of the Dundee City Mouse Police
Pipe Band.

Thank you for buying another in the series of

The Brechin Tales

Hamish and the Marvellous Set of Bagpipes

You may well recall that all was not well in the old city of Brechin, even more so in the McMoosie household. Hamish was still very sad over the tragic loss of his one and only set of bagpipes. And as everyone knows, it is a most terrible thing for a piper who plays in the Keltic Moosie Pipe and Fiddle Band to be without his pipes. The bagpipes had become Aunt Maude had said, 'Attached to the pointed end of my long black umbrella with the goose head handle.'

The result of the accident was that the bagpipes were broken beyond repair. Hamish comforted himself with the fact that at least Aunt Maude had now gone back to her home in Edzell castle and had taken her umbrella with her.

There was only one thing to do, Hamish thought sadly, and that was tp put the pipes away in the store cupboard. They would never be played again.

Hamish could not bear the thought of parting with his pipes. This time instead of just dropping them on the floor, he gently wrapped the pipes in tissue paper, placed them in their special cardboard box and lifted them carefully onto the shelf in the store cupboard. If only, Hamish thought to himself, I had done this before my pipes would not now be broken beyond repair.

"My pipes...my pipes..." thought Hamish sadly.

A big salty tear fell from Hamish's eye and trickled down his cheek. He sniffed and wiped it away quickly with the back of his paw.

Hamish decided that there was only one thing to do and that was to go up into the City and see Alisdare MacBrymer the bagpipe maker. MacBrymer would make him a new set of pipes.

The pipe maker lived under the Kindly Grocer's shop on David Street, with a collection of hairy Scottish spiders.

MacBrymer always remarked that it was a very good place for any mouse to live. He had lived under the grocer's shop for longer than any of the mice folk could recall.

Rumour had it that he was probably older than Hamish's Aunt Maude, and as all knew, she was very old indeed.

Food was always left out for MacBrymer, especially pieces of fine Arran cheese, by the kindly grocer who was a friend of Bill the gardener. The two friends, gardener and grocer, had an understanding of nature and Moosie things. Once a week the pipe maker had a real blow-out feast when the Kindly Grocer left out a slice of Arran Cheese and a little of the delicious Meat Loaf that Willie his assistant made every Wednesday. A slice of Willie's Meat Loaf on a Brechin Heckles followed by a smidgen of tangy Arran cheese, washed down with a cup of dandelion tea was pure heaven.

Alisdare MacBrymer

Hamish came into the shop just at the right time; MacBrymer was making his morning cup of tea. Before Hamish had time to say 'Good Morning' the old bagpipe maker looked up from pouring the milk into his cup of tea. He poured a second cup.

" I suspect, Hamish McMoosie, that you have come about a new set o' pipes. I hear tell that yours' met with some kind of accident."

3

Hamish sighed, and picked up the cup of tea that old Alisdare pushed across the workbench towards him,

"No chance of a biscuit to go with the tea, I suppose?"

The biscuits were duly passed over and Hamish selected one of his favourites, a crisp Abernethy. He was about to dip the Abernethy in his cup of tea but thought it would be better not to do so. You see Abernethies have a habit of breaking up when dunked in tea and would leave a kind of brown Abernethy sludge at the bottom of the cup. Dorma was always complaining to Hamish that when she came to put the dirty cups in her dishwasher she always found a soggy mess at the bottom of H a m i s h ' s mug... leftover A b e r n e t h y Sometimes, when Dorma was looking the other way, or was doing something else about the house, Hamish would stick his long whiskered nose in the cup and lick up the soggy Abernethy with his

"Hamish thought Dorma did not know of his habit of dunking"

4

tongue. He thought that in this way Dorma would not know of his habit of dunking. But typically for Hamish he always got things wrong. It was a very good plan, to lick up the soggy mess at the bottom of the cup, but unfortunately small pieces of the soggy Abernethy had a habit of sticking to his whiskers. Although she never said a word, Dorma always saw the wet crumbs sticking to one or more of her husband's twitching whiskers.

The pace of life for the mice folk of Brechin matched the style of the slow country life led by the City's humans. There was always time for a chat, always the time of day to be passed when one went into a shop. There was a need to know who had won what prize in the local flower show: what new shop might be opening on the High Street, and of course most important of all to Brechin folk, mice and human alike - how did Brechin City football team get on in the last game they played?

However, and it was a big 'however', in Alisdare MacBrymer's bagpipe shop, it was politics that had to be aired, before things were bought. The old bagpipe maker coughed a gently little cough so as to make sure that he had Hamish's attention,

"I hear that the Scottish Parliament is considering putting a tax on Forfar Bridies, and Arbroath Smokies."

Old MacBrymer left the words hang in the warm air of his shop and sipped his tea. Hamish who had just taken a bite of his crisp Abernethy spluttered,

"Eh! What! Where did you hear that rubbish MacBrymer, they would never dare."

"I hear that the Scottish Parliament is considering putting tax on Forfar Bridies"

Hamish waited for an answer. He saw that the pipe maker was slowly dunking his Brechin Heckles biscuit in his cup of tea. Almost right in, Hamish noted. Perhaps Heckles did not break up when dunked. Hamish thought that he might possibly try dunking one of the Brechin-made biscuits later. Normally Hamish spread his Heckles with butter and strawberry jam and did not dunk them in his mug of tea.

"Perhaps Heckles did not break up when dunked"

"Heard it from my cousin, the pipe maker in Edinburgh, who heard it from a senior Civil Servant mouse, who overheard it during a meeting with the Moosie Member of Scottish Parliament for the Isle of Mull. Seems that the new parliament building is costing so much money that new taxes might have to be raised to pay for it."

"But Bridies, and Smokies! No never. It is beyond belief."

Hamish, who found himself in dire need of another biscuit, having finished his Abernethy, reached over for a Brechin Heckle. As he reached for the tin the pipe maker snapped the tin lid shut,

"Now what was it that you were wanting Hamish? No time for more tea or biscuits, I have a business to run."

The whole matter of the possible taxes on Forfar Bridies and Arbroath Smokies was dropped. Hamish, who was not very up on things political, resolved to himself that he would take up the matter with Inky MacWriter the editor of the local paper. He and Hamish often sipped a damson wine together at the Haggis and Neeps Inn. Inky, being the editor of a newspaper, would know thought Hamish.

Inky MacWriter the Editor

Hamish decided to get back to the business of why he had come.

"I want a new set of pipes, please. To replace my old ones, that is."

"By 'New' Hamish do you mean, 'New' or do you mean 'New to you, but second hand to me?"

"He wished he had an Abernethy
to help him think"

This question posed by MacBrymer set Hamish a problem. He had not really considered the practicalities of whether to buy a brand new set, which of course would have to be made, or to buy a used set of bagpipes. Then of course there was the cost of the pipes to consider. He wished he had an Abernethy to help him think, even a Heckles might help his brain work out what to do.

"Well?" remarked Alisdare MacBrymer kindly.

Hamish thought. He knew that the Keltic Moosie Pipe and Fiddle band had a wedding engagement at the Northern Hotel the coming Saturday, then there was always the Ceilidh night on Fridays at the Haggis and Neeps Inn. He doubted very much if Alisdare MacBrymer could make a new set in just five days.

"How long will it take to make a brand new set, if I was to order one?"

"Hamish jumped up and ran around in circles"

"I could make you one in about a month, there's a lot to do in the making of a set of pipes Hamish me lad."

A month! That was of no use at all. Hamish let out a sorrowful squeak. What on earth would the Keltic Moosie Pipe and Fiddle band do without their piper, Hamish wondered frantically.

Hamish jumped up and ran around in circles, filling the shop with his quivering voice. Three of the spiders that had just finished their morning cups of tea, fell out of their webs and landed in a tangled heap of legs on the top shelf.

"Now stop that running around in circles and squeaking like that. You are giving my spiders a headache".

MacBrymer caught hold of Hamish's kilt as Hamish ran round him for the fifth time and hauled him back.

"Thinking of Wailing MacSquawk are we Hamish? He would love to fill your place with the band..?"

MacBrymer chuckled to himself. He had a liking to tease people in a good-humoured way. MacBrymer really had no time for MacSquawk who was a boastful sort of character. MacSquawk was always telling

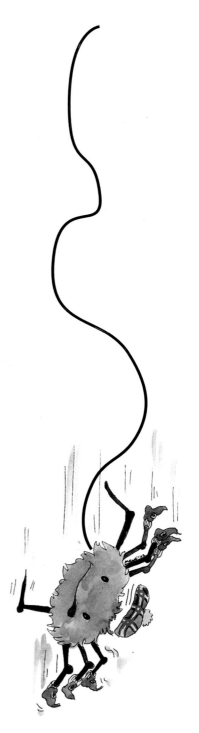

"Wailing MacSquawk"

people that he was the best piper in the county of Angus. Hamish, however, (who really was the county's best piper) never bragged about his ability to play the pipes.

On the top shelf the spiders, who had now untangled themselves from their collective twenty-four legs were deep in conversation. They too had heard Wailing MacSquawk play and were in no hurry to repeat the experience!

Hamish admitted to MacBrymer that he was indeed thinking of MacSquawk and that MacSquawk would take his place. A whole month would give that poor excuse for a piper, Wailing MacSquawk just the chance he was looking for to take over Hamish's piping for the Keltic Moosie Pipe and Fiddle Band.

MacBrymer was scratching his whiskers and tapping a foot impatiently waiting for Hamish to settle down and make up his mind on whether to order a new set of pipes. The old bagpipe maker's eyes strayed to the shelf above his workbench and an idea formed in his mind. The shelf held all sorts of bits and pieces of bagpipes, chanters, flutes, and even a dusty old accordion. As it was rarely used, the spiders had made their webs up there and raised their children in peace. The pipe maker vaguely recalled that somewhere amongst the clutter should be a brown leather bag with the Tayside Mouse Police Crest emblazoned on the outside.

" I can't possibly wait a month for a new set. I just can't!" burst out Hamish at last.

Hamish stood dejectedly, his whiskers drooping, his ears folded over and his long tail curled tight up. Alisdare tut tutted and coughed a little cough.

"There is a chance that I may be able to help you, Hamish, in the short term that is, and only if you are considering buying a new set of bagpipes.If only I could remember where I put that bag."

"What bag is that?"

"The one I put up on the shelf, the one with the Tayside Mouse Police crest emblazoned on it."

Hamish muttered that he could not see how a bag could help with the problem. It was a set of bagpipes he needed, not a bag, even if it did have the Tayside Mouse Police crest emblazoned on it. The pipe maker scratched his whiskers and thought. He knew that he had put the bag somewhere. Then he remembered…

"Right Hamish there is only one thing to do. Its up on my workbench for you my lad and you will have to look on that shelf for me."

"Hamish climbed up on the workbench"

Avoiding a sharp pair of tailor's scissors that Alisdare had inadvertently left laying open Hamish climbed up onto the workbench. The spiders looked down and feared the worst. They were not to be disappointed. Hamish could see all the bits and pieces that cluttered the shelf. Bits of this, bits of that. A tin or two containing who knows what, and at the back behind a large dented tin of Abernethy biscuits Hamish saw a dusty brown leather bag which had a crest on the outside. He reached in, moved the Abernethy biscuit box to one side and was disappointed to find that it was easy to move: it was obviously empty. With one paw he

"The dust caused Hamish to sneeze"

grasped hold of the bag and pulled it to the front of the shelf. Dust flew everywhere. The spiders took refuge in the top right hand corner of the highest of their webs. The dust caused Hamish to sneeze, and as he did so he lost his grip on the bag. The bag fell from the shelf and landed with a thud on the workbench. The spiders fell out of their webs and landed in a tangle once more. They held a hurried, hushed conversation that centred on moving out of the shop to somewhere more peaceful.

Hamish lost his footing and he fell onto the bench too, but he landed on the brown leather bag with the Tayside Mouse Police crest on it. Hamish heard a sort of a wheeze and then a gurgling soft wail that came from something inside the bag. The spiders began to pack their bags. It was all too much for them, falling out their webs and all the noise and dust!

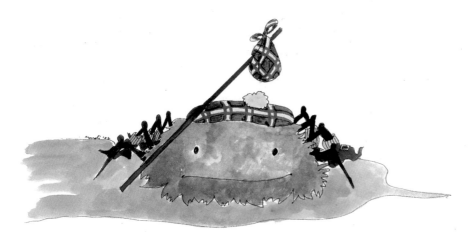

"The spiders began to pack their bags"

"Hamish! What have you done? I hope that what is inside that bag has not met with a similar accident to your pipes. Let me see. Move over, move over."

Hamish moved over and rubbed his bottom. He had landed right on the spot where Aunt Maude used to poke him with her long black umbrella with the goose head handle. He brushed a spider's web from his left ear. The web got caught up on his paw. As much as he tried to shake it off it stuck firm. After much wiping of his paw with a duster he found on the bench, the web fell off.

"Double bother!"

"What did you say Hamish? Stop playing with that spider's web and muttering to yourself and come and help me."

Using the duster he had found on the bench Hamish helped Alisdare MacBrymer to wipe the dust from the bag. When it was clean the pipe maker opened the bag and peered inside. Hamish heard Alisdare muttering to himself, and poked his head inside as well.

"Get your head out of this bag Hamish, you are blocking the light. Ah! Yes all seems well. Now lets have a look on the workbench."

MacBrymer carefully lifted out a bundle of something wrapped in an old copy of the Brechin Advertiser. The bundle was solemnly placed on the workbench and the wrapping unfolded.

Hamish's eyes grew wider and wider, his tail which had remained curled up since the news that a new set of bagpipes would take a month to make, sprang straight out, his whiskers bristled. Lying before him he saw the most wonderful set of bagpipes,

"Now Hamish, I want you to try these bagpipes out, just in case your fall damaged them. These pipes are very special."

While Hamish sorted out the chanter and the drones and started to inflate the bag by puffing very gently MacBrymer went on to explain just why the pipes were so special. He told Hamish, who was only half listening as he was concentrating on inflating the pipe's bag, that the set of pipes had been made by his grandfather for Sergeant Ernest MacBlast, the founder and pipe

"Sergeant Ernest MacBlast"

18

"Hamish spread the drones, put the bag under his left arm, placed his claws on the chanter's holes, and played"

major of the very first Tayside Mouse Police Pipe Band. Of course in those days it was called the Dundee City Mouse Police Pipe Band, there being no such place in those days as Tayside. Sergeant MacBlast was renowned all over Scotland for his skill with the pipes. His rendering of 'Westering Home' played in jig time would bring tears to an audience's eyes. The Sergeant had finally retired and had come to live in Brechin. After his death some twenty years ago his widow had brought the pipes into the shop to sell. Police widow's, MacBrymer explained, did not get much in the way of a pension in those days, and he had given her a good price for the pipes. Why it must be all of the twenty years since he had set his eyes on the pipes.

"Eh! What's all that? What are you chattering about?" wheezed a red faced Hamish MacMoosie.

"Oh, nothing, nothing at all. It is just the ramblings of an old man. Now Hamish give us a tune and let hear how they sound after all this time in the leather bag."

Hamish spread the drones, put the bag under his left arm, placed his claws on the chanter's holes, and played.

A tear formed in the right eye of Alisdare MacBrymer the bagpipe maker as he heard the wonderful sound of 'Westering Home', being played in jig time.

"A tear formed in the right eye
of Alisdare MacBrymer"

MacBrymer said Hamish could borrow the old pipes until his new pipes were ready and that suited Hamish very well. Even though the pipes were old and dusty, when Hamish blew into them, they sang out like new.

The spiders however had made up their minds. After forty years of peaceful living in Alisdare MacBrymer's bagpipe shop they moved out and caught the next bus to Dundee.

GLOSSARY

Ceilidh
: A gaelic word (pronounced "Kay-lay") for a Scottish dance party with traditional dancing, music and fun.

Smidgen
: A word meaning a small piece of something.

Abernethy
: A traditional and popular Scottish biscuit first made to a Recipe of Dr Abernethy. Hamish's favourite served with a cup of tea and "dunked".

Forfar Bridies
: An oval shaped meat filled pasty rather like a Cornish pasty but without vegetables except for onion. Named after the small town of Forfar but popular all over Scotland.

Arbroath Smokies
: A type of lightly smoked small haddock with unique flavour. Arbroath is a small coastal town on the east coast of Scotland.

Brechin Heckles
: A semi-sweet biscuit unique to the town of Brechin where Hamish lives, made in the shape of a tool used in the Jute Industry which once flourished in the region. Made by MacKays the Bakers, Brechin. Hamish thinks Heckles are best spread with butter and jam, or with a slice of Willie's meatloaf.

Dorma's Abernethy Biscuits

This recipe has an especially buttery taste which Hamish loves
5 ounces of Plain Flour
4 ounces of best Scottish Butter
3 tablespoons of sugar
1 teaspoon of cream of tartar
Half a teaspoon of bicarbonate of soda
1 tablespoon of milk
1 pinch of salt

Sift the flour, salt, bicarbonate of soda and cream of tartar together.
Rub in the butter to the flour mixture until the mixture looks like bread crumbs.
Stir the sugar into the milk until it dissolves and then add it to the flour and butter mixture.
Form the mixture into a stiff dough.
Roll out the biscuit dough on a lightly floured board to a thickness of about half a centimetre and cut out 10 round shapes with a plain cutter.
Prick each biscuit all over with a fork.
Place the biscuits on a greased baking tray.
Bake in a pre-heated oven at 350F or 180C for 15 minutes.

enjoy

Note

In Dr Abernethy's original 19th century recipe he added Caraway seeds to the Abernethies which were said to help digestion. If you want to do this add about half a level teaspoon of caraway seeds to the flour mix.

The Fourth Brechin Tale

Hamish and the Quest for the New Spirtle

The Brechin Tales

Hamish and the Quest for Dorma's new Spirtle.

Dedication

This tale is warmly dedicated to all those who make
Porridge in the traditional way

and to

The Gordon Highlanders.
Long may their memory be cherished.

Terry Isaac

Hamish and the Quest for Dorma's new Spirtle.

Christmas and New Year had come and gone, and it was the second of January. The snow that had started to fall on Christmas Eve, and had continued to snow on most days since then, was thick on the ground. Roads were almost impassable, and certainly down in the Channonry the Wynd was most definitely blocked. Hamish saw that Roderick, the human writer who lived in the old house, could not get his old red Jaguar out of the garage, and chuckled to himself.

"That's no car for this weather, not at all. A four by four is what he should have."

The mice folk of Brechin did not suffer as much as the human folk during bad periods of winter weather. They either stayed indoors; used the secret tunnels that led under parts of the city or were clever enough to make sure that their cars were four by fours. Hamish, being very patriotic, had bought an Inversnecky Vehicle Organisation, Sutherland Overland Limited Edition four wheel drive the previous year. The IVO Company of

Inverness made the only car in Scotland designed especially for mice. In fact they were the only Scottish mice-car makers and resisted being taken over by the big car makers. Hamish often proudly announced, to anyone who cared to listen, that the IVO was the best car in the world. 'Big is not always a sign of quality'. Of course, he would add that his IVO had never let him down, as yet.

More to the point of our tale, Hamish decided, on the second of January, that it was time he replaced the spirtle he had broken on Christmas Eve. Dorma, his wife, flatly refused to make porridge without a spirtle with which to stir the porridge while it was cooking. Hamish, having broken her spirtle, could not very well complain: even though he loved his morning porridge more than any other breakfast cereal. Hamish had looked all  over Brechin, even the Hardware Store on David's Street could not help, and they sold just about everything one could imagine. So Hamish thought that he would motor over to Montrose and buy Dorma her new spirtle. He was sure to find one in Montrose he told himself.

The Inversnecky Vehicle Organisation Jeep excelled itself. It made easy work of the many snowdrifts and did not slip and slide too much on the snow-covered road. Montrose was busy. Mice folk from all around were attending the sales; catching up with friends after the New Year break, or just shopping. Hamish parked by the Corner House Hotel. It was owned by a friend of his who had served with the First Mouse Gordon Highlanders but was now retired and ran the Hotel.

Partan MacFlan was a huge mouse. One could always tell by his manner that he had been a soldier. Like a lot of big mice, underneath his fierce exterior he was very gentle. Any ex-Gordon Highlander can tell you just how gentle Sergeant Majors really are, especially when drilling recruits on the Parade Square at the Bridge of Don Barracks, in Aberdeen, the home of the regiment.

Partan MacFlan

Hamish decided it was far too early for a glass of Damson Wine, of which he was known to partake when visiting the Corner House Hotel. Also, Hamish reminded himself, he was driving and that if one was driving one should not drink alcohol. A cup of coffee would be fine instead and Hamish thought Partan would be sure to know where to buy a spirtle.

"Any ex-Gordon Highlander can tell you just how gentle Sergeant Majors really are"

"Spirtle, Hamish, spirtle?... Well now let me think...,"

Thundered Partan MacFlan from the other side of his bar counter.

Hamish sipped the strong hot coffee that Partan had made and waited.

"Mmm. Spirtles eh? That poses a question in this day and age. I suppose they still make them. Although, I think that the lassies these days do not know how to make good porridge!"

Partan began to muse aloud,

"As I remember, it was Malaya '62... we had a superb Indian Mess Cook called Sam who made the finest porridge I have ever tasted. And he used a spirtle to stir the porridge! Fine spirtle he had with a carving of an elephant's head on the handle. Teak wood I think. Bless me, I can almost taste that porridge now. His porridge was famous all over the Far East.

The Colonel of our Regiment even tried to get him to work in the Officer's Mess, but no, he stayed true to us did Sam. Sergeant's Mess man through and through..."

"Hamish sipped the strong hot coffee that Partan had made and waited"

31

'Oh dear,'

Thought Hamish to himself,

'Once Partan starts on about his army life he will never stop. The shops will be closed by the time he finishes.'

Partan's wife rescued Hamish from a long, long army tale. She was a Shetlander who stood no nonsense and had that ex-Regimental Sergeant Major under a firm paw.

"Partan! Stop that blethering! You know full well that you always say my porridge is the equal of no other. Now Hamish, you need to go to the top of the town to the Hardware Shop, they will sell them. Off you go. I need Partan to do some dusting."

Hamish escaped from Partan's ramblings about Malaya and Indian army cooks. He had to walk from one end of the town to the other so as to reach the Hardware Store. He doubted if the shop would have a a spirtle as Tam in the Hardware shop in Brechin would have said to try their store in Montrose. On the way he decided to call in at one or two other shops; he thought might have spirtles.

"Stop that blethering..."

The first shop he tried was noted for its bargains. He looked among the pots and pans. He looked among the cooking and kitchen tools. He looked everywhere, up and down and around and around. He found wooden spoons of all sizes, rolling pins, wooden steak hammers, but no spirtle. In desperation he asked the young assistant who was filling up the shelves.

"I'm looking for a spirtle. Do you sell them?"

She looked at him in amazement, "Spirtles! What are they when they are at home then?"

"Do you not know what a spirtle is lassie?" Said Hamish, somewhat rudely.

"A spirtle's a long wooden pin that one would use to stir porridge while it cooks."

"Don't like porridge, so I don't cook the stuff. Try up the street." Replied the lassie.

Hamish ambled off up the street muttering to himself about the awful fact that men, mice and children were most probably being sent out their front doors to work, or to school, without their porridge if lassies like that did not cook porridge. On a cold winter morning nothing was finer than to feel the comforting warmth of a hot bowl of porridge sitting easily in ones tummy. Half out loud he muttered,

"Folk should rise up and demand porridge for breakfast,"

Folk in the street looked round in amazement.

He would start a Movement, he told himself. Yes, a movement that was it. A name came into his mind 'To Eat More Porridge' or TEMP for short. Hamish could visualise TEMPS everywhere. Posters calling for TEMPS would be seen, in the oil companies in Aberdeen, in the Mills in Dundee and in the halls of power of the Scottish Parliament.

He would put advertisements in the Brechin Advertiser, the Dundee Courier and 'The Voice of the North' the Press and Journal. His advertisement would be simple and to the point 'TEMPS NEEDED - apply Hamish McMoosie'. Hamish was still dreaming of the worldwide domination of TEMPS when a voice called out,

"Watch out Hamish! Watch where you are going! What are you doing in Montrose at this time of a morning?"

Cran MacAchan put out a kindly paw to save Hamish walking off the pavement and into the path of an oncoming StrathTay bus.

"Oh, good morning Cran. I am trying to buy a spirtle for Dorma, to replace the one I broke on Christmas Eve. I just cannot seem to be able to find any. This is getting to be a hard task Cran, a hard task indeed. I have not had a bowl of porridge for a week or more."

Hamish saw hundreds of bowls of steamy, smooth porridge floating before his eyes and sighed,

"Double bother, oh double bother."

Cran MacAchan was an old friend of Hamish. They both played in local fiddle bands and often practised together. Cran put an arm round his friend's shoulders and tried to cheer him up,

"Come, come Hamish it is not like you to be so down and sad. Let's go find a spirtle together. I'm sure with my help you can find one. A mouse without his morning bowl of porridge is a sad mouse indeed. Lets be moving along."

Hamish felt much better to be in the company of Cran and was sure that his quest for Dorma's new spirtle would go well. The pair set off up the street. Cran said that they should try in the Community Shop first, they seemed to have most things and would surely have a spirtle. As they walked along chatting away Cran spoke about John MacCheeser, the owner of the delicatessen shop in Forfar,

" Hamish, I know that your favourite drink is damson wine but have you tried the new wine John has in the store - Elderberry? My, that's a fine drop of stuff that is. Smooth, almost a black red. Goes well with a smidgen of Mull cheese. Almost one might say like port, yes port that's it. Have you tried it?"

Hamish admitted that he had not, and added that right at the moment he had more important things on his mind than Elderberry wine, good, or bad. It was a new spirtle that was uppermost in his thoughts,

"Tell me later Cran, later. I cannot think of anything else other than a new spirtle."

Cran opened the door of the Community Shop and went in, Hamish followed. The shop was full of interesting things. Prints of Montrose, neatly framed; aromatic oils for use in candle burners, pottery items, toys, Celtic jewellery, books and all sorts of useful odds and ends. The two friends looked around the shop, but nowhere could they see a spirtle.

"Can I help at all?" Asked a small delicate mouse assistant.

"Um er, a spirtle. If you know what a spirtle is ",

Hamish replied his head deep in a box of wooden spoons, rolling pins, wooden pegs, and salad forks.

"I ken well what a spirtle is! I'll have none of your patronising of me Hamish McMoosie. I ken you well; Dorma's my Mother's Aunt's kin. Aye and I know what you did to her fine spirtle that was her Mother's and her Mother's before. Shame on you, using it to prod the snow indeed. A spirtle's for porridge nothing else."

Hamish hung his head. Cran tried to look as if he was not with Hamish.

"And you Cran MacAchan, you just stay still. I know you two are together."

Cran was about to speak but thought better of it. Small and delicate, Rosie St Cyrus may be, but she had the measure of them both. Hamish coughed as if to clear his throat,

"Hamish hung his head"

"Cran tried to look as if he was not with Hamish"

"Rosie, I am sorry. It's just that I cannot find a spirtle and everywhere that I have been today, it's the same story. Either there are no spirtles, or they say 'What's a spirtle?' Or the lassies say that they do not even cook porridge!"

"Aye, that's as well maybe. You see Hamish the girls now are not brought up to cook as we had to do. All they have to do is pop down to the supermarket and buy instant porridge and pop it in the microwave. There's even freshly made pots of porridge available, just heat and serve."

Rosie nodded somewhat wisely.

"Instant porridge, heat and serve. Mercy me. What ever next?"

Hamish was amazed. Dorma soaked the oatmeal over night and boiled and simmered the porridge the next morning until it was smooth and creamy. It took over an hour. Heat and serve! Microwave! His Dorma would have not contemplated the idea. The problem was (thought Hamish) that Rosie had not said if she had any spirtles,

"Have you a spirtle Rosie?"

"No Hamish I do not have any spirtles. I stopped selling them over six months ago. Nobody wants spirtles any more. Try Highland Scene down by the Corner House Hotel. They sell them to tourists."

Cran reminded Hamish that they had started out just by the hotel and now had to walk all the way back. Hamish was not to be put off by Cran's remark.

"Well if Rosie says that that is where we will find spirtles we had better go and check. We have nothing to lose and maybe a spirtle to win."

So off they set back the way they had come. Cran suggested that it might be better to look in shops as they passed by, rather than go all the way back only to find no spirtle and having possibly passed by shops that did have them. They went into the Co-op. Nothing. A newsagent's - again nothing. In desperation Hamish suggested that they try Boots the chemist,

"Boots Hamish?! It's a spirtle we are after not cough mixture."

At last, after many fruitless enquiries, they came to 'Highland Scene'. The shop sold and hired kilts and all manner of Highland clothes. One could find just about any clan tartan in the shop. If it was not in stock there were catalogues to browse through. The shopkeeper was a fund of information on styles, colours, dress codes and which type of sporran should be worn for what occasion. He knew exactly which sort of shoe or sock should be worn. All in all anyone wanting to buy or hire would always come away satisfied even if they had to wait a day or so for an order to be delivered from the catalogues.

"Morning Hamish. Morning Cran. What can I do for you today?"

Robin McDresswell beamed at the two friends.

Hamish was looking round to see if a spirtle was hidden among the sporrans and socks, but he could not see any. Cran, the bolder of the pair, piped up,

"Robin, Hamish is looking for a spirtle. Don't happen to have any about the place do you?"

"That I do Cran. That I do. A good range as well. Five different types."

"What! Oh me. I'm saved. Porridge again! Wonderful!"

Squeaked Hamish with delight, his tail curling, and uncurling.

Mr. McDresswell reached behind a rack of tartan ties and pulled out a big china jar that was overflowing with spirtles.

"Here we are. Take a look at these Hamish."

Hamish stood in wonder at the number of spirtles standing like soldiers at attention in the jar. Some had carved thistles, others a small deer head, some a hairy spider and some a round haggis as their head; one even had a goose head. Hamish left that one alone. They all had a piece of Tartan ribbon tied round them to show that they were Scottish. At least that is what Hamish thought.

A spirtle with a thistle head was selected. The one Hamish had broken had something similar carved on one end. He held it in one paw. It was well balanced. He twirled it round as if stirring a pot of porridge. Hamish put the spirtle up to his eye and looked along the length, it was nice and round and smooth. It seemed to be just what he wanted. The price too that was just right, two pounds and seventy-five pence,

"Yes this will do nicely Robin. It's a fine example of Scottish craftsmanship. Must have been made in Inversnecky or some such Highland city. It's fine just fine."

Just then Hamish noticed a label tied to the spirtle and with growing concern read out what was printed,

"Made in China from Mongolian pinewood."

"Eh! What's this Robin? 'Made in China from Mongolian pinewood!' What ever next?"

"Now, now Hamish do not judge everything by the label. You said yourself that it was just fine. Shall I wrap it for you?"

Hamish considered what he should do. The spirtle looked fine. It felt right in his paw. The wood was smooth and well turned and the thistle looked

"A very fine spirtle!"

just like a thistle should look. He decided that he had to ask if Robin had any spirtles that were made in Scotland,

"Do you have any made in Scotland, Robin? This one looks fine but I would prefer a Scottish one if that is possible."

McDresswell explained that it was the lack of suitable pinewood that made home produced spirtles a rarity. New forests were being planted, but it would be some years before any home produced spirtles would come onto the market. He went on carefully spelling out the need to plant more forests, and not just pines but oak, elm, beech, sycamore. For many hundreds of years the Scottish forests had been cleared for industrial use. It was now time to replace the open spaces with new plantations. Trees hold the earth together, give shelter to the birds, and in their shade animals can make their homes on the forest floor, or in the trunks of the trees.

"So in a way Hamish by importing spirtles now, from places that have trees to spare, we can help our own forests to grow. See on the label it states that for every tree cut down one is planted and China has many square miles of good forest. Like you I would prefer home produced goods, but these are of good quality and are made by local communities. We are helping them as well as they are making goods for us. I also hear tell that down in Edinburgh the government is bringing out a new scheme to encourage local craftsmen to produce Scottish spirtles, but it may be some time before that happens."

Soon the Chinese spirtle was wrapped in a bright tube of blue and white paper. Hamish handed over the two pounds and seventy-five pence. He still felt that a Scottish spirtle would have been better but considered that the proof would be in Dorma's porridge the next morning. Hamish waved goodbye to Cran and made his way back to Brechin along the snow - covered roads.

Hamish opened the front door and called out to Dorma that he was back. He could hear his wife in the kitchen, singing to herself as she worked. A wonderful smell drifted from the kitchen, through the house and into the hall where Hamish was standing taking off his anorak and wet boots…the smell was of a steak pie cooking in the oven. His whiskers twitched with the thought of the golden crisp pastry, of the tender meat in rich, dark brown gravy. Dorma's steak pies always went down well with those who ate them, especially Hamish. He heard Dorma calling,

"Lunch is ready Hamish, you have come home just at the right time. There's steak pie, with boiled potatoes, carrots and cabbage. Wash your hands and come and set the table."

Dorma always made sure that Hamish had lots of vegetables and salads. Although she made mouth-watering puddings more

"A wonderful smell drifted from the kitchen"

often than not, Dorma always put fruit out on the table. Hamish busied himself laying the kitchen table,

"Oh Dorma I have bought a new spirtle to replace the one I broke. I hope you like it. I'll put it on the work surface."

"Thank you Hamish. I am sure it will be just fine. I'll try it out in the morning when I cook your porridge."

Hamish smiled his little smile and thought, 'Porridge in the morning.'

And there was. A steaming bowl of creamy porridge that when eaten, warmed Hamish through and through. He even had room, well just, for a small second helping. He noticed that Dorma was looking at her new spirtle; she turned to her husband and smiled,

"Hamish did you know that the Chinese make their breakfast porridge from rice? I wonder how they found out about our Scottish Spirtles?"

Hamish wondered indeed!

The End

Dorma's Real Scottish Porridge

for each serving you will need:
1 cup of water
2 rounded tablespoons of oatmeal
(this is NOT the same as porridge oats)
Salt to taste
Basins of creamy milk or cream

Put the water in a heavy bottomed saucepan and bring to the boil. When boiling, add the oatmeal by sprinkling it onto the boiling water whilst stirring with your spirtle. (You can make do with the handle of a wooden spoon if you do not have a spirtle). When the porridge has come to the boil reduce the heat to the lowest setting and simmer porridge for 20 minutes or as long as you like. Some cooks simmer porridge slowly overnight.

Add salt <u>only</u> when porridge is cooked (salt may harden the oatmeal and stop it from swelling) and simmer for just 5 minutes more.

Ladle into serving bowls and serve with individual bowls of cream or creamy milk. Dip each spoonful of hot porridge into the cold cream or milk before being eaten.

In the Highlands of Scotland porridge was traditionally eaten standing up from wooden bowls using a horn spoon but Hamish always eats his porridge sitting down.

A true Scot never, never adds sugar!

enjoy

GLOSSARY

The Channonry   The cathedral area in the old part of the city of Brechin.

The Wynd   Narrow walled 800 year old street in the Channonry.

Brechin   Old city in the county of Angus, Scotland.

Montrose   Coastal town in Angus, Scotland.

Inversnecky   Local name for the city of Inverness, capital of Highland Region.

Spirtle   An old traditional kitchen tool made from a piece of wood, about 25cms in length used to stir porridge whilst it cooks.

Gordon Highlanders Very famous Scottish regiment of foot soldiers which in 1994 amalgamated with other Scottish Regiments to become The Highlanders.

Shetlander   A person from the Shetland Islands. The Shetland Islands are a group of about 100 islands situated North of the Scottish mainland. Fewer than 20 of the Islands are inhabited.

Blethering   Scottish dialect word meaning to talk nonsense.

Ken   A Scottish dialect word meaning 'understand'. As in 'You ken what I mean'.

Fact

In China they do make a type of porridge from rice known as
Congee or *Jook* which like true Scottish porridge is
best cooked very slowly.

THE ADVENTURES OF
HAMISH MCMOOSIE

NEW EXCITING ADVENTURES TO COME ...